# SPACE ✦ PIRATES

# Stowaway!

swung his telescope to follow the
spaceship. It was a huge black galleon with
billowing sails. At the back of the ship,
leaning out over open space, was a long
silver plank. Sam grinned as he saw the
white skull-and-rockets flag flying from
the topmost mast. *Space pirates!*

Look out for more
stories of swashbuckling
space adventures in

# Stranded!

# Mutiny!

# Treasure!

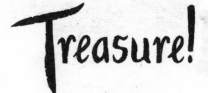

# SPACE PIRATES

# Stowaway!

## JIM LADD

Illustrated by
Benji Davies

nosy
crow

## With special thanks to Paul Harrison
### To John Joe — the first pirate to join the crew

First published in the UK in 2013 by Nosy Crow Ltd,
The Crow's Nest, 10a Lant Street, London SE1 1QR, UK

Nosy Crow and associated logos are trademarks and/or registered
trademarks of Nosy Crow Ltd

Text © Hothouse Fiction, 2013
Illustrations © Benji Davies, 2013

A CIP catalogue record for this book is available from the British Library

Printed and bound in the UK by Clays Ltd, St Ives Plc

Papers used by Nosy Crow are made from wood grown in sustainable forests.

ISBN: 978 0 85763 154 1

www.nosycrow.com

# Who's who in
# COMET'S CREW

SAM
STARBUCK

CAPTAIN COMET

BARNEY

PEGG
AND
LEGG

# Who's who in
# BLACK-HOLE BEARD'S CREW

BAGGOT

YARR

BLACK-HOLE
BEARD

# Chapter One

# CRASH LANDING

Samson Starbuck peered through the telescope into outer space, watching spaceship rocket boosters flicker across the night like fireflies.

"How many planets are there in the Fudo system?" asked Professor Argon, his holographic teacher.

Sam set the telescope to zoom in on the distant constellation, but as he did, a spaceship entered his planet's atmosphere. Checking that Professor Argon wasn't watching, Sam swung his telescope to follow it. His parents were meant to have been back ages ago, but this spaceship wasn't his family's sleek silver cruiser. It was a huge black galleon with billowing sails and golden portholes, out of which jutted enormous cannons. At the back of the ship, looming out over open space, was a long silver plank. Sam grinned as he saw the white skull-and-rockets flag flying from the topmost mast. *Space pirates!*

"Samson?" Professor Argon asked again. "How many planets?"

"Errr, three?" he guessed.

"Very good," Argon said, pointing a transparent arm up at the distant worlds. Mum had changed the holo-teacher's settings back to "humanoid" again, so he had two arms and two legs like Sam, but his programming was universal so that he could resemble any of the species that he taught. Sam liked it best when Professor Argon was a three-headed Fishoid, but Mum said his holographic drool was too distracting.

3

"Glooton 5 is famous for its jelly mines. Half of all the jelly eaten in the universe comes from that one wobbly planet. The more you study," said Argon, adjusting the glasses perched on his computer-generated nose, "the more you realise that the sky is filled with incredible worlds."

"Yeah," sighed Sam, "but this planet isn't one of them. P-Sezov 8 is just a lump of rock."

He wasn't even exaggerating. The entire planet was covered with a thick blue stone that nothing could grow on. There were no plants or animals, and there were only two places on the entire planet where people lived, and one of them was his parents' lab.

His holo-teacher flickered as his program selected the right file. "Actually, P-Sezov 8 does have one special function – it is ideally placed for exploring all the amazing worlds around it."

Sam rolled his eyes and nodded. That was why his parents, Castor and Stella Starbuck, had based their lab here – so that they could travel all round the cosmos collecting samples of plant life and

still be home in time for tea. Sam usually got to travel with them, but sometimes, like today, his parents insisted that he stay at the lab and catch up on his schoolwork.

Sam had begged them to take him with them – they were off to find the rare biting moss of Pretoid Alpha and he'd always wanted a pet – but instead they'd programmed the professor, and told him they'd be back before his lessons were over.

"And of course," Argon continued, "P-Sezov 8 is also a known port for space pirates, who use its convenient position to launch attacks, raids and treasure hunts across the galaxy."

The space-pirate ship was now close enough for Sam to hear it flying low over the lab. Sam watched through the window as it travelled over to the other side of the planet, where laser beams were criss-crossing in the sky. Fireworks flared here and there, and if Sam concentrated hard enough he could just about hear the noise of fighting and the raucous singing of popular space shanties. The ship was heading for Pirate Port.

Sam had always wanted to go there and see a real space pirate up close, but his parents had banned him from setting foot on that side of the planet.

"Space pirates are dangerous," Mum had insisted. "It's not all space shanties, swashbuckling and bowling, you know. There's squabbling, stealing and duels to the death."

So Sam was stuck on the most boring planet this side of the Milky Way and he wasn't even allowed to go to the only interesting place on it.

Sighing, Sam watched the pirate ship disappear from sight. He was about to turn away from the window when something else caught his eye. Amongst all the flashes and streaks in the sky over Pirate Port, there was one speck of light that seemed brighter than the others. The longer he stared at it, the bigger it seemed to get. Sam grabbed the telescope again and focused the lens. It was still there and getting bigger by the second. *What was it?* It looked too small for a ship and it was moving too quickly.

Then he realised – it wasn't getting bigger, it was getting closer – and it was heading straight for the lab!

"Samson, are you listen— Eek!" Argon's voice turned into a high-pitched squeak as Sam dived right through his body and flung himself under a desk,

curled himself into a ball and waited for the impact. The only sound he could hear was the rapid beating of his heart as it hammered away inside his chest. Then there was a bright flash and a piercing howl as the object streaked past the window, followed almost immediately by an enormous explosion. The force of the strike shook the lab.

Sam waited until the ringing in his ears had stopped, then he crawled out from under the desk and had a quick check that he was OK. His legs seemed to work and he still had ten fingers to waggle, so everything seemed in order. He raced downstairs to see what had happened, and looked out on to what used to be his garden.

Where there had been a stretch of rock and a large telescope, now there was a huge crater with thin wisps of smoke curling over the rim and a few shards of stone stuck into the side of the laboratory. In the middle of the wreckage was a satellite dish, knocked off by whatever had crash-landed. *Oh great*, thought Sam. *That's killed the*

*Stowaway!*

*holovision. Although that does mean no more boring Professor Argon!*

Sam peered over the edge of the crater. There, glowing at the very bottom of the hole, was a small, shiny metal sphere. He scrambled down inside the crater and picked it up.

He'd seen something like this before... but where? It looked a bit like the homing beacon on his parents' spaceship. In fact, it looked *a lot* like the homing beacon on his parents' spaceship.

With a sinking feeling, Sam realised that it *was* the homing beacon from his parents' ship! But where was the rest of the ship? And where were his parents?

# Chapter Two

# SOS!

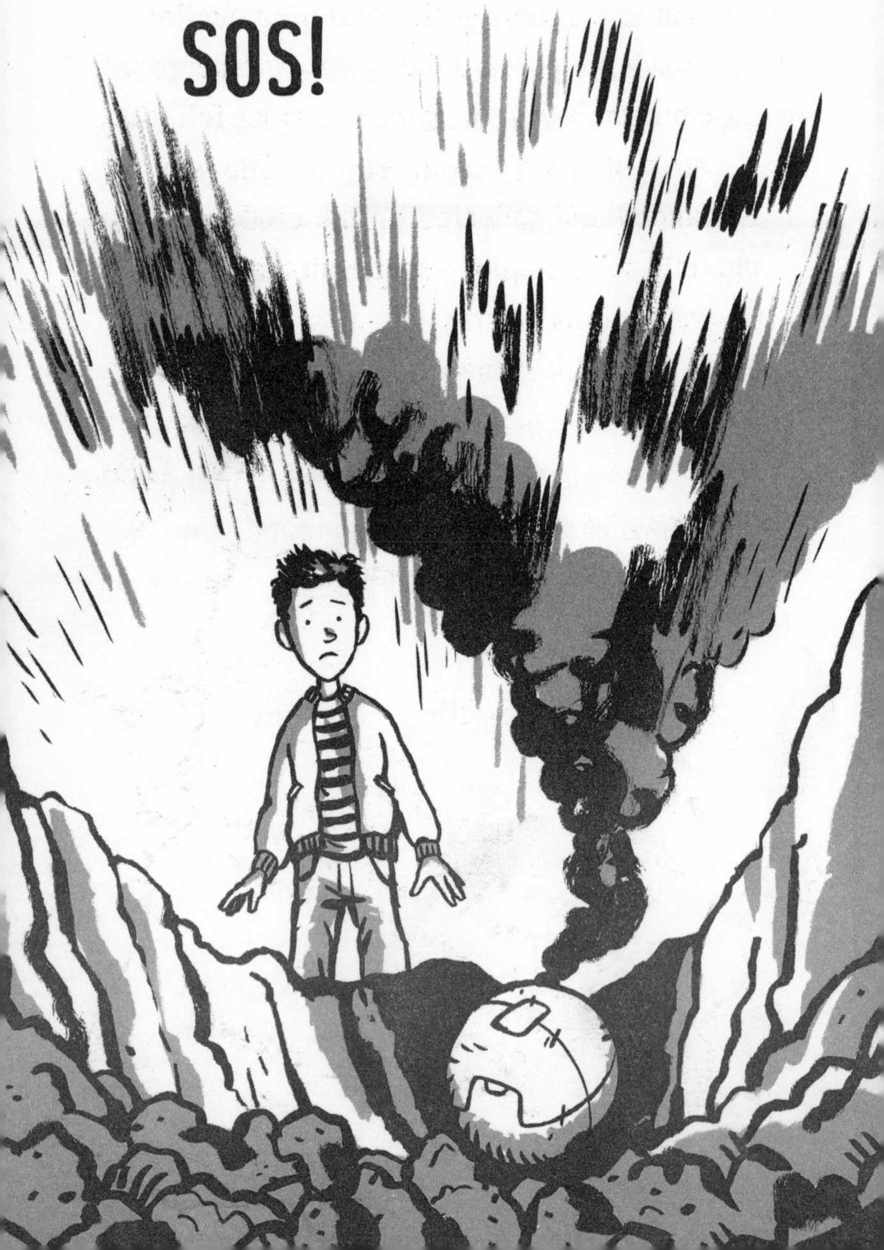

# Stowaway!

Sam stared at the small ball that had crash-landed in his garden. Ignoring the fluttering feeling in his stomach, he pressed the beacon's emergency release button. With a *ftzzt* the two sides fell apart and a strip of silvery cloth fell out. The way the light danced and reflected on the cloth meant it could only be one thing – spacesuit material. And there was writing on it.

Stella Starbuck's handwriting was impossibly neat and tiny, which was handy as she had written quite a lot on a small scrap of cloth. Sam's hand was shaking as he tried to read what the note said.

SAM - DON'T PANIC.
SOMEHOW WE'VE CRASH-
LANDED ON PLANET X.
YOUR DAD IS BLAMING THE
NAVIGATION SYSTEM - BUT THEN
HE WOULD, WOULDN'T HE. GET
HELP. MUM XXX
P.S. REMEMBER TO WASH
BEHIND YOUR EARS
P.P.S. AND EAT YOUR GREENS!

Sam turned the cloth over. On the other side was a sketchy drawing of various planets and stars.

*A map showing the way to Planet X! But that's impossible!*

Everyone had heard of Planet X – it was said to be a whole world made of solid gold. For hundreds of years, space pirates across the galaxy had searched for the planet – each hoping to make their fortune – but none had ever found it.

"Computer on!" yelled Sam as he tore back into the lab. His parents had always drummed into him what to do in an emergency. He rushed over to the main computer console. "Computer, activate the interstellar SOS message." He scanned the map his mother had drawn, and added it to the message.

"Send," he commanded with relief. Now every rescue team on every planet in the solar system would be rushing to find his parents. Just knowing that there was a plan of action made Sam feel better.

"ERROR," came the computer's mechanical voice. "NO SIGNAL. MESSAGE COULD NOT BE DELIVERED."

*No signal?* thought Sam, confused. *But how...?*

Then he remembered the wrecked satellite dish. He looked around for Professor Argon, but he had already deactivated. Suddenly Sam felt horribly alone. He never thought he'd miss his holo-teacher. Without a satellite signal he couldn't contact anyone, not even to tell the authorities about the crash. His grandparents were only on the next moon – but suddenly that felt like a galaxy away.

There was no rescue team based on P-Sezov 8. There was only one spaceship and his parents had it. Sam could feel his mouth going dry and his hands getting sweaty.

He leaned against the window sill and rested his forehead on the cool glass. The fireworks were still flickering over Pirate Port. The only other people on the planet... were the space pirates.

*Maybe the pirates could take me to the next planet so I can contact Interstellar Rescue?* Even as he thought it, Sam realised it wouldn't work. Space pirates spent all their time avoiding the authorities, not looking for them. That's why

14

they stayed on P-Sezov 8, away from everything and everyone.

*But Mum and Dad aren't just stranded anywhere – they're on Planet X, a planet made of gold...* An idea formed in Sam's head as he looked at the scrap of cloth in his hand. *Space pirates would do anything to find Planet X... and I've got a map showing the way!*

# Chapter Three

# PIRATE PORT

# Stowaway!

Sam had stuffed some clothes into a bag and jumped on his hoverbike before he had really thought through what he was about to do. So when he arrived on the outskirts of Pirate Port he suddenly felt bottom-wobblingly nervous. He started to wonder whether this was such a good idea after all... But his parents needed him and this was his only way of helping them. Sam's boots clanked as he stepped determinedly on to the metal walkways of the port, and into what felt like a different world.

The first thing he noticed was the smell – a combination of rocket fuel, spices, dirt, and the sickly scent of grum, the space pirates' favourite drink. Then the noise hit him. The dock was teeming with people and creatures. Sam could see aliens from all around the galaxy, some species he'd only read about and some he didn't recognise at all!

A spider-bodied Arachnoman clattered by on eight peg legs. A fat Chubbertron from the planet Largus waddled past, blinking its twenty eyes.

A huge, hairy, one-horned Minocerous carried a massive wooden trunk casually on one shoulder. Minoceri were famously bad-tempered, so Sam made sure he didn't get in its way. Unfortunately, as he was watching out for the Minocerous, he walked straight into the back of a gigantic, semi-transparent blue Squart. With a sloppy squelch he pulled himself off the Squart's sticky skin.

"Sorry, sir," stammered Sam as the slug-like

Stowaway!

alien turned and swayed above him menacingly.

"How dare you!" came a high-pitched voice in reply. "First you grab my bottom and then you think I'm a man. I've never been more insulted!"

The Squart lady slid off, leaving Sam sticky and a little bit confused. He tried to brush the blue goo off his coat as he walked forward. But as Sam turned the corner he stopped in amazement, sludge dripping messily off his fingers, and gazed up at the ships docked in front of him.

There was every size of spaceship imaginable, from small moon schooners to massive interstellar galleons, all held in place by their gravity anchors. The biggest ships towered high above the dock, their masts stretching for the stars, some with sails already unfurled to catch the solar winds.

Sam stared from one ship to another. He'd never dreamed he'd be able to see real space-pirate ships up close! The *Spacehorse* was sharp, pointy and fast-looking – and its fearsome number of laser cannons suggested that you didn't want to mess with it. The *Galaxy Maiden*

was a sturdier affair: at first glance Sam thought it was a cargo ship – until he spotted the holes in the side which hid the weapons and the skull-and-rockets flag flapping lazily from the top of the mast. The elegant *Siren of the Stars* came next, its chrome surfaces glinting in the light and everything stored neatly on deck.

Then came the *Jolly Apollo*. Sam never thought he'd find a space-pirate ship disappointing but even he had to admit that the *Jolly Apollo* was a sorry-looking vessel. It squatted by the dock like an exhausted Phyraxian toad, battered, dirty, and covered in patches of rust and space algae. It looked unlikely to make it to the end of the port, never mind sail the solar seas. It was the exact opposite of the final ship, *Gravity's Revenge*, which sat menacingly at one end of the walkway completely dominating the dock. Sam recognised it as the one that he'd seen go past earlier. It was a huge space galleon, painted deep black and bristling with golden laser cannons. No ships were moored anywhere near it, and Sam could see why. It was completely terrifying... *and* the coolest thing Sam had ever seen in his life!

Looking at ships wasn't going to help his parents though. Sam needed to find a captain to ask for a lift to Planet X. He leaned on a large barrel of grum and looked around the dock. *If I were a space-pirate captain*, he thought, *where would I be...?*

The sound of singing drifted across the dock.

21

Opposite Sam was a building with the words YO HO BOWL picked out in neon lights. He wandered over and peered through the grimy window. Inside, pirates were singing space shanties and knocking back foaming tankards of grum. And all of them – even the ones with peg legs – were wearing bowling shoes. The clatter of falling bowling pins rattled behind them.

"Strike!" someone yelled.

"I'll strike you!" another voice replied. There was the sound of laser cutlasses being fired up.

Sam gulped. He stood as tall as he could and tried to look as confident as possible. He marched to the door and was just about to go in when a yell echoed around the dock. "FIGHT!"

Before Sam could move out of the way, the doors to the bowling alley burst open and everyone ran out. If there was one thing pirates loved more than bowling it was a good fight. Sam was carried along by a rush of bodies, all eager to get a view of the action. Eventually he got to the edge of the crowd surrounding the battling pirates. In front of him arms and legs were whirling and fists and tentacles were flying – much to the entertainment of the crowd, who shouted encouragement.

"Hit him, you useless swab!" someone yelled as a giant three-legged monster chased a group of smaller shipmates. Another was clinging on to a crab-clawed buccaneer and slapping him with a bowling shoe. They were the dirtiest fighters Sam had ever seen. One pirate was even bashing another one over the head with a small accordion, which made screechy "whee-whaa" noises with every blow.

KABOOOM!

The loud retort of a laser musket echoed around the dock. Instantly the fighting stopped and the crowd fell silent. The knot of onlookers parted as a huge pirate strode into the centre of the circle. He was tall – at least two and a half metres high – and as broad as a barrel of grum. A thick beard as black as the night sky itself spilled halfway down his chest, tangled and twisted like a living thing. The ends were plaited and held in place

23

with thick red knots that looked suspiciously like they'd been dipped in blood. A long scar stretched across one cheek and the one eye not hidden behind a patch burned with an evil glare. In one hand he held a laser musket. On his shoulder sat a small, mean-looking bird with a curvy beak.

A deep hush settled on the dock. All Sam could hear was the faint "whee-whaas" coming from the accordion as one end bounced up and down like a tired yo-yo. All the pirates who had been fighting stood still as statues, frozen in the positions they were in when the musket went off. A Kraken – a many-tentacled alien a bit like a giant squid – held a couple of pirates at arm's length as if he wasn't sure whether to drop them or not, and a Minocerous held a two-headed opponent in a double headlock. All eyes were turned towards the menacing pirate that stood in the middle of the circle.

"Shiver me space boots," whispered an elderly pirate next to Sam. "It's Black-Hole Beard!"

# Chapter Four

# FACE-OFF

"What's this, me hearties?" roared Black-Hole Beard to the group of pirates. "A little bit of sport before we sail? Who's that you're scrappin' with? Is that the crew of the *Jolly Apollo*? Blisterin' barnacles, don't waste time fightin' that sorry sack-load o' starfish!"

There were sniggers and snorts of laughter from the watching crowd. The odd creature on Black-Hole Beard's shoulder shook its feathers and started to sing:

"There once was a pirate ship
That looked like a right old tip
You should never follow
The *Jolly Apollo*
Cos the captain's a proper big drip. *Squawk!*"

"Arr, that's right, Baggot, me beauty," smiled Black-Hole Beard. He looked at the Minocerous. "Yarr, put him down. You might catch something."

"Arr!" the Minocerous replied, dropping the two-headed alien on the metal walkway with a clank. It jumped up and scuttled over to join the rest of its crew. One of its heads was smiling while the other looked furious.

"Why, thank you," said the happy head.

"I'm warning ya, horn face," said the angry one. "If you've scuffed my bowling shoes I'm going to stick that horn of yours right up ya—"

"Do not fear, my boys – your captain has arrived!" A voice was heard from the back of the crowd as a tall, thin figure started to squeeze his way through. "Excuse me... excuse me... yes... could I just... oh, pardon me, madam... excuse me, coming through there..."

Eventually he reached the front, where he paused to brush down his clothes and reposition his hat.

He was a tall, flamboyant-looking character, with a bottle-green coat and huge frilly shirt cuffs. He had a long moustache which was waxed into extravagant curls at the ends and he had three eyes, two of which were covered with eye patches.

"Well, well, if it isn't Calamity Comet," Black-Hole Beard sneered.

"That's *Captain* Comet, if you don't mind," Comet replied, twirling his moustache. Although he was trying to sound brave, Sam saw him flinch when Black-Hole Beard scowled at him. Captain Comet was just as scared of the huge pirate as everyone else. Comet's crew, which included the two-headed alien and the Kraken, hurried over to stand behind him.

"And what a surprise," Black-Hole Beard continued. "You've missed the fight *again*. So what was it this time? Hiding, or could ye not find your way? I wouldn't trust you to navigate your way out of bed without getting lost!"

The crowd around Sam burst into laughter.

28

"Hiding?" Comet blustered. "*Lost?* I have travelled to the furthest reaches of the galaxy! *And* I've found my way back!"

Black-Hole Beard snorted in disgust.

"You call me a coward," Comet continued, "yet I have weathered cosmic storms, cheated certain death in asteroid fields and evaded evil aliens."

"You tell him, Cap'n!" cried one of his crew.

Comet seemed to be growing in confidence. He pointed a finger in the air and declared, "Nothing scares Captain Joseph Hercules Invictus Comet!"

The crowd gave an encouraging round of applause.

"Is that a fact, me hearty?" asked Black-Hole Beard. The clapping stopped immediately. Sam watched as Black-Hole Beard slowly walked over to Comet. His crew took a step back, leaving Comet on his own. Black-Hole Beard leaned down until his face was so close that his beard looked like it was tickling Comet's nose. He glared into Comet's one good eye. A thin trickle of sweat ran down the side of Comet's face. Everything was quiet and tense, and Sam realised that he was holding his breath.

"BOO!" shouted Black-Hole Beard, sending Comet springing backwards in fright. At the same time Black-Hole Beard flicked his laser-cutlass through Comet's belt. Comet's trousers promptly dropped to his ankles, displaying his bright, flowery underpants for the world to see.

Black-Hole Beard threw back his head and roared with laughter, his gold teeth glinting in the starlight.

"Nice bloomers, Comet!" mocked Black-Hole Beard. The crowd howled with delight. Comet, red-faced, hauled his trousers back up.

"Actually," muttered Comet, "these were part of some booty I seized."

Black-Hole Beard let out a deafening guffaw. "Would this be the booty you then lost?" he sneered.

"Yes... regrettably so," said Captain Comet. "We were attacked while we were all eating dinner – which, as you know, is *totally* against the pirate code."

"Bah!" spat Black-Hole Beard. "The pirate code! As I sees it, the pirate code only applies to *pirates*. You and yer crew are a bunch of mummy's boys."

Black-Hole Beard grinned as the crowd laughed at Comet. Then he held up his arms for silence. "You're a lily-livered planet-lubber, Comet," he snarled, his eyes bright pinpricks of hate. "Crumbling cuttlefish, I've seen space slugs with more backbone than you! You're no pirate – you're just a waste of a good eye patch."

That was an insult too many for Comet.

"I'll show you!" he cried. "I'll show you all that I'm no planet-lubber!"

"Oh, will you now?" Black-Hole Beard replied, his voice a low, menacing whisper. "And how are you planning to do that?"

"Well, I'm, I'm, I'm..." Comet seemed to be floundering a bit. "I'm going to..."

The crowd leaned forward in expectation – as did the crew from the *Jolly Apollo*.

"I'm going to... find Planet X!"

This caused gasps from the crowd, and, Sam noticed, from the *Jolly Apollo*'s crew. Sam's heart jumped in delight. *This was perfect!*

An evil sneer slipped across Black-Hole

Beard's face like a slash from a sword. "Planet X? You can barely find your own poop deck," he snarled. He turned to his crew. "Avast, me hearties, back to the *Gravity's Revenge* – it's time for pirating, not gossiping."

With Black-Hole Beard gone, the entertainment was over, so the crowd seeped away too. Comet's shoulders slumped.

"Planet X," he wailed. "What was I thinking of?"

"Captain, are we really going to find Planet X?" asked the Kraken eagerly.

Comet dragged a hand slowly down his face. Even his moustache had drooped.

"Back to the ship," he muttered.

"Er, excuse me!" yelled Sam as the pirates trudged back to their ship. *Of all the ships in the port it had to be the* Jolly Apollo, he thought as he raced after Comet and his crew.

"Hey!" Sam called again as Comet walked up the gangplank. Comet whirled round to see who was talking, his bottle-green coat twirling

through the air behind him.

"Um, Captain Comet," Sam started, suddenly finding himself tongue-tied at talking to a real, live space pirate. "I, um..."

"Spit it out, boy!" Comet commanded.

Sam gave up. "Can I come with you to Planet X?" he asked.

Comet looked at him for a moment, then sauntered back down the gangplank.

"Tell me – does this look like a cruise ship to you?" he asked.

Sam shook his head. It didn't look like much of a ship at all, but he wasn't about to say that.

"Indeed, that's because it's not. So sorry, sonny – *we don't take passengers*." Comet started back up the gangplank.

Sam put his hand in his pocket and held on to the map. "But I could be useful," he called.

Comet spun round again and arched an eyebrow.

"Useful? You could be useful? Pray tell how. Can you tie a Pangorian bow-switch knot, for example?"

"No," Sam replied.

"Then perhaps you can hit a Lupillian dust rat with a hand blaster from a cable's length away?" asked Comet.

"Errmm, no," replied Sam, who had never held a hand blaster or even heard of a Lupillian dust rat.

"Ah, I see. Then can you operate a pan-dimensional compass and reverse magnetic stellar binnacle?" asked Comet.

"Err, no," Sam replied meekly. "But—"

"Then you're no use to me!" Comet exclaimed. "I'll make this very clear. I don't have planet-lubbers on my crew – and even if I did I wouldn't take a scrawny runt like you. Now, be quiet or you'll get a taste of my sword."

Comet went to grab the hilt of his sword for emphasis, but there was no sword there. He patted a couple more times then frantically searched all round his waist.

"Oh brilliant!" shouted Comet. "Just brilliant!

Now someone's gone and thieved my sword. You can't trust *anybody* round here!"

And with that he whirled away and stomped up the gangplank and on to the *Jolly Apollo*, leaving Sam alone on the dockside.

Sam stood there, stunned. His only hope of rescuing his parents had just disappeared up the gangplank with Comet. He hadn't even had a chance to mention the map. Sam had to get on that ship. If Captain Comet didn't want him on board, then he would just have to make sure Comet didn't *know* he was there. If he couldn't be a passenger, he'd have to be a stowaway...

Chapter Five

STOWAWAY

Sam sat down on a barrel of grum and watched as the *Jolly Apollo* crew started hauling cargo aboard, singing a lively space shanty about a haunted bowling alley. The only way on to the ship was up the gangplank, but Sam knew there was no chance of sneaking up there without being spotted.

Suddenly a deafening roar engulfed the dock. *Gravity's Revenge* was setting sail and its rocket boosters had just blasted into life. The ship spun slowly from its berth until it was pointing in the opposite direction, then rose majestically into the sky, its great sails billowing as they caught the solar wind. Two loud BAZOOMS rattled across Pirate Port as the *Revenge* fired a laser-cannon salute. Then, with a low rumble from the ship's boosters, it was gone.

On the dock, everyone continued about their business, used to seeing ships come and go, but Sam was amazed – this was *so* much better than watching the ships from his bedroom window! He watched until the *Gravity's Revenge* was little more than a speck in the distance, then he looked back at *Apollo's* crew carrying their supplies on board.

That was it!

If he could hide himself in one of those crates he would get carried right on to the ship! All he needed to do was wait until the coast was clear.

Sam watched as the crew of the *Jolly Apollo* went up and down the gangplank. As well as the Kraken and the two-headed first mate, there was a small jelly-bodied pirate who left a slimy trail behind him, a fearsome-looking Snippernaut with gigantic lobster-like claws, picking up three crates at a time, and a furry creature with more mouths than Sam could count. More pirates worked below deck, and deep inside the ship Sam could hear the muffled *kerthunk* of bowling

39

balls hitting pins.

Then came the moment he was waiting for – all the crew were below deck at the same time. Sam knew he wouldn't have long, so he took his chance and sprinted across the deck and dived behind the pile of crates. Just in time! As Sam peered around the crate, the huge Kraken swung into view, its metal-tipped peg legs clanking down the gangplank. To Sam's horror it stopped right in front of the box he was hiding behind. Sam jumped back as one of the Kraken's thick tentacles snaked past him and around the bottom of the box. But instead of picking it up, the Kraken lifted the lid and plunged a tentacle inside. There was a disgusting smell and the sound of a tentacle being pushed into something squelchy. Then a satisfied slurping and guzzling.

Sam carefully peered
around the box and saw the
Kraken pull a slimy ball of glugspawn
out of it. The pirate tossed the foul blob
into its beaky mouth and noisily chomped
it down. Then it gave a huge belch, looked
over its shoulder guiltily and let the lid fall
shut. The tentacle slid away, and the Kraken
picked up another box and clattered back up
the gangplank.

Sam hoped that glugspawn wasn't the only
food on board. But there was no time to worry
about that – he needed to get into one of the
crates before the Kraken came back. With all his
strength he pulled on the lid of a big metal box to
the side of him, but it was locked. So was the lid
on the next box, and the next.

All the lids were nailed tight. He began to panic
– if he couldn't get into one of these crates he'd
never get aboard. But he knew there was one that
was open...

41

Groaning, Sam lifted the lid a crack and was almost knocked backwards by the terrible stench of the glugspawn. It was like someone had mushed rotten fish into a cat's litter tray. Could he really hide in there? The sound of pirates shouting on board the *Jolly Apollo* made his mind up for him. He quickly climbed into the crate and slid into the stinking, slimy, jelly-like eggs. The smell was overpowering and the gloopy mess soaked into his clothes and slid down the back of his neck.

"Where's Barney gone?" came a hoarse-sounding voice from outside the box. "I thought he said he would load these crates on board?"

"Said he had dinner to cook," another voice replied.

"Dinner! Is that what he calls it?" the gruff pirate snorted. "I wouldn't feed it to my Tangorian Desert Hound."

Suddenly Sam felt his box move jerkily into the air. The gloop slopped around, washing over Sam's head as he was carried along, then dropped with a thud. Sam was drenched in glugspawn

42

goo but he held his nose and kept quiet. No way was he going to be found now. There were more thumps as other boxes were dropped nearby, then came the unmistakable sound of Captain Comet's voice.

"Everything on board?" he asked.

"Aye aye, Captain," came the reply.

"Excellent – then raise the anchor!" shouted Comet.

"Aye aye, Captain," repeated the crew.

There was a grinding clunk as the gravity anchor was raised.

"Set the main sails," ordered Comet. "Rocket boosters on standby."

Sam felt the *Jolly Apollo* shudder as a low, rumbling sound reverberated from below.

"Mr Pegg, Mr Legg, fire the salute!" shouted Comet. Sam remembered the two-headed alien from earlier on. Sure enough, two voices replied, one sounding grumpy, the other seeming nicer.

"Aye aye, Captain," they called.

BAZOOM!

Sam waited for another shot, but it didn't come.

"It's two shots, you zoodle-brains!" shouted Comet.

"The blasted laser cannon has jammed again!" complained Pegg.

"What? I thought I told you to get it fixed!" exclaimed Comet.

"You told *that* useless barnacle, not me," snapped Pegg, nodding towards his other head.

"Now, now, me hearty, we both know the captain told *you*, not me," said Legg.

"You're both the same person!" shouted Comet in absolute exasperation. "Whoever said two heads were better than one obviously hadn't met you!"

Sam heard the sound of someone stomping up to the laser cannon.

"Right, let me have a look," Comet huffed. "There! I've told you a hundred times, you've got to check the firing mechanism is free of obstructions. You... just... need... to... pull...

this... there! Right, now the trigger just needs a light press and..."

BAZOOM! BAZOOM! BAZOOM! BAZOOM! BAZOOM!

"Help! Make it stop! Make it stop!" shouted Comet.

BAZOOM! BAZOOM! BAZOOM! BAZOOM! BAZOOM!

There was a loud clunk as something heavy landed on the deck near Sam's hiding place, shaking up the spawn and releasing a new load of stomach-churning stink.

"Captain – I think you've blown up the Yo Ho Bowl," one of the pirates whispered.

"Don't be ridiculous," snapped Comet.

Even from inside the crate, Sam could hear shouts and cries from Pirate Port.

"Oh. Oh dear," Comet muttered. "Ermmm, right. OK. Rocket boosters to maximum, please. Get us out of here. And someone fix that bit of mast back on."

Footsteps disappeared across deck followed by the slam of a cabin door. The deep rumble from somewhere down below changed pitch as the rocket boosters cranked into action, only to be followed immediately by a loud backfire. Then the engines spluttered into life and Sam felt the *Jolly Apollo* lurch upwards and away.

Buried deep in a box full of stinking glugspawn, Sam smiled to himself – he was on his way to Planet X!

# Chapter Six
# CABIN BOY

Sam had to get out of the crate! He was desperate to see what was going on and the glugspawn was getting *everywhere* – up his nose and in his ears. Breathing was tricky, but he didn't dare open his mouth in case he swallowed some of the eggs. If they smelled this bad, Sam couldn't imagine how horrible they'd taste. Soon he couldn't take it any longer – he opened the lid a crack and took a gulp of air. Through the gap Sam could see the crew of the *Jolly Apollo*, squabbling and fighting as they worked on the deck.

"Hey, you moon-headed numbskull – watch what you're doing with that mop!"

"Put your back into it, you four-legged shirker!"

The pirate with two heads was even arguing with himself. "Call that a knot? Me granny knits stronger knots that that!" said Pegg.

"*Your* granny? I think you'll find she's *my* granny!" Legg replied.

Something hit Sam's box with a dull *thunk* as the pirates started throwing things. Sam raised the lid a little higher to get a better look, but as he did the box lid gave a loud CREEAAAKKKK. The fearsome-looking Snippernaut who was working on deck immediately spun round. Sam dropped back into the slime in a flash.

*Did he see me?* Sam wondered in a panic.

A second later the box lid was flung open and light flooded in. *I guess he saw me*, Sam thought as a large claw descended and grabbed him by the shirt. Sam hung in the air, dripping glugspawn on to the deck. The Snippernaut's face loomed in front of him, his antennae twitching.

"So what's this then?" snarled the Snippernaut. "A stowaway, is it? Well, I'm sure the captain will be interested to meet you. CAPTAIN! CAPTAIN! There's something here you should see."

"What's wrong now?" demanded Comet as he burst from his cabin. "Can't a man have a nap – I mean, plot a course – without being disturbed every two minutes?"

"Stowaway, Captain!" the Snippernaut replied, holding Sam at claws' length. "A stinky one."

49

"A stowaway, eh?" said Comet.

The Snippernaut let Sam go and he fell to the deck with a bump. Sam could feel the eyes of the crew watching as Comet loomed over him. It seemed like Comet could too, because he bellowed so that everyone could hear.

"You again, eh? Well, let me tell you, Captain Joseph Hercules Invictus Comet does not tolerate stowaways! Do I, me hearties?"

The crew roared in response.

"There's only one punishment fit for stowaways, isn't there, me hearties?" Comet continued.

The crew yelled their approval. Sam swallowed.

"That's right – hang him from the ship-shape!"

A confused silence settled over the *Apollo*.

"No, that's not right," Comet muttered. "A-ha! I mean hang him from the yardleg!"

"Do you mean the yardarm, Captain?" asked Sam.

Comet looked wide-eyed for a moment.

"That's right, me hearty – I see you didn't fall for my trick. Well done!" Comet blustered. "Well, let's get on with it!"

"Sorry, Captain, but we've not had a chance to fix it since you shot it off earlier," shouted the Snippernaut, pointing at the tangled mess of shattered pole and rigging heaped on the deck.

"Oh good grief," sighed Comet. "Why is nothing straightforward? Right then, we'll go old school. Boys, let's make him walk the plank!"

The crew cheered and parted, leaving a route from Sam to the side of the ship, where a plank jutted out from the edge of the ship into the emptiness of space. Sam thought quickly.

"Surely it's against the pirate code to just make someone walk the plank?" he said desperately. "I mean, you don't know why I'm here – I might have been trapped in that crate, or kidnapped or anything."

"You're right, it would be against the code," said Pegg, leaning so close that Sam could smell what he'd had for breakfast. And his breakfast didn't smell nice. "But the code is for pirates, and *you* ain't a pirate."

Comet pressed a button on the handle of his replacement cutlass and with a crack the edges of the sword glowed with bright laser power.

"But, but..." Sam stuttered as he edged away from the flaming sword.

Sam thought desperately. He had

to let Comet know about the map, but he couldn't tell him about it in front of the whole crew; the fewer people who knew about it the better. "Can we go somewhere and talk about this, Captain?" he asked.

"The only talking you'll be doing, lad, is with *this*!" Comet replied, thrusting the sword at him.

Sam edged backwards on to the plank. He was suddenly very aware of the black nothingness all around him. The plank wobbled like a diving board, and Sam felt his knees go weak. Comet stood at the edge of the ship, his crew around him shouting, jeering and waving their fists.

Sam gulped. "I've got a proposal," he said as firmly as he could.

"Oh really – and why would I be interested in that?" sneered Comet, waving his laser cutlass menacingly from side to side, and nearly dropping it overboard.

Sam shuffled towards Comet.

"You're meant to go the other way!" Comet said in surprise, still waving his cutlass.

Sam slid close enough to whisper in Comet's ear. "I know where Planet X is!" he hissed.

"Ha! Nice try – now time to say goodbye!"

"Wait!" Quickly Sam plucked the map from his pocket. "I do – look, I've got a map!"

Comet stepped out on to the plank with Sam and looked suspiciously at the scrap of cloth.

"My parents are scientists, and they've crash-landed there," Sam explained. "They sent this to me in a homing beacon."

Comet sidled up closer, flipped up his two eye patches and peered closer at the map with all three of his eyes.

"And that's genuine, is it?" asked Comet in a conspiratorial whisper.

"Yes," replied Sam. "Just think, with this *you* could be the pirate that finds Planet X. That would show Black-Hole Beard."

"Pass it here," said Comet.

"No!" Sam snatched it away. "If I did that, what's to stop you from pushing me off the plank? If you want the map, I come along too."

"Hmm – you drive a hard bargain." Comet stroked his moustache.

"'Ere, Captain, is everything all right?" shouted one of the pirates from the deck.

Comet looked alarmed, as if he'd forgotten the crew were watching. Quickly, he flipped his eye patches back.

"OK, it's a deal," said Comet under his breath.

"Wait – how do I know I can trust you?" asked Sam.

"I swear on the pirate code!" Comet hissed.

"But I'm not a pirate, remember," said Sam.

"You are now!" Comet spun round to face the crew. "Arr, me hearties," he announced, pulling Sam down on to the deck next to him and putting his arm around him so that Sam's face was smushed up into his armpit. "Your old captain has a kind heart and is an easy touch for a sob story. This snivellin' wretch has lost his parents – much like your captain himself. So I've taken pity on the lad and made him our new cabin boy!"

A cheer erupted from the crew.

"But if he's a lazy swab I'll throw him to the quasar sharks!" shouted Comet to an even louder cheer.

"Now, we must give our new shipmate a proper pirate welcome – let's break open the grum and do some bowling!"

And that got the loudest cheer of all.

Chapter Seven

# CAPTURED!

# Stowaway!

Sam was woken the next morning by the snores of his fellow crew members. He could still taste last night's grum. Sam had always wondered what grum was like, and he'd been quite surprised to find out that it was really just lemonade milkshake – very sweet and fizzy – and, as Captain Comet had told him, it was great for keeping away space scurvy.

If last night was anything to go by, space pirates certainly loved their space shanties. There had been at least thirty-seven verses of a "Yo Ho Ho and a Bottle of Grum" and a full and noisy attempt at "Ninety-Nine Bottles of Grum on a Wall". No wonder everyone was still asleep. Sam looked around at the swaying anti-gravity hammocks floating around him.

Suddenly a loud blast echoed around the ship. Immediately all the pirates stirred. With moans and grunts, they jumped out of their hammocks and started walking to the door.

"Is that a foghorn?" Sam asked the pirate nearest to him.

"Nah, that's breakfast," he replied, pulling his trousers over his peg leg.

"Barney's meals always come with a warning," joked another.

"Who's Barney?" asked Sam.

"He's the ship's cook. Now, look lively or there'll be none left."

Sam followed the pirates to another low room. Inside was a long table with benches on either side. There were bowls laid out and the pirates were already tucking in. Sam found a space and sat down.

When he looked into his bowl, he wished he hadn't bothered. It was filled with a lumpy sludge. To say it was grey would be insulting to that colour, which was a vivid and exciting shade compared to the disgusting mess in Sam's bowl. A bubble of gas rose to the surface of the mess and burst with the sound of a wet fart. Then something moved inside it.

"Aargh! What was that?" shouted Sam.

The elderly pirate next to him laughed and the

air whistled through the gaps in his teeth.

"That'll be a weevil worm," he said. "Occasionally they fall in the cooking pot. Not bad tasting, as it happens. Hey, lads – cabin boy's got a weevil worm!"

The other pirates groaned with disappointment.

"Beginner's luck," one grumbled.

Sam didn't feel too lucky. Or hungry.

"You can have it," he said, pushing the bowl to the pirate.

"Arrr, thanks mate!" he replied before wolfing down the sludge, weevil worm and all.

Just then Captain Comet entered, wearing an

even more elaborate outfit than yesterday. His long coat had even frillier sleeves, and the buckles on his boots shone so brightly it hurt your eyes to look at them.

"Ahoy, me hearties!" he announced. "Your brilliant captain has wonderful news!"

The chatter in the mess room died down as everyone turned to look at Captain Comet. Soon the only noise was the slurping of sludge.

"Last night," Comet began, lowering his voice dramatically, "the ghost of Long John Starseeker appeared to me." There was a gasp around the hall. "He spoke to me, one glorious captain to another, two brave buccaneers together—"

"Get on with it!" someone shouted.

Comet held his hands up for silence. "And he told me the way to Planet X!"

The whole mess hall erupted into cheers. Someone threw their breakfast in the air and grey sludge rained down like wet, sticky confetti.

"All right, you lazy sons of space slugs!" Comet shouted. "This is no time for sitting round gossiping like old women – we've treasure to find!"

The crew cheered, and bowls and spoons clattered down as pirates rushed to get up on the deck.

"Not you, Cabin Boy," said Comet, putting a hand on Sam's shoulder. In seconds the mess hall was empty, and Comet brought out the map.

"I thought Long John Starseeker had told you the way?" asked Sam innocently.

"Yes, well." Comet looked flustered. "Pirates like a good tall tale, lad, and if you were a *captain* you'd know that." He cleared his throat. "Anyway, thanks to the map I've managed to plot a course."

"Ooh, did Long John Starseeker give that to you?" came a voice from behind them. Captain Comet and Sam whipped round. Barney the Kraken was holding a stack of bowls in one of his tentacles, and using the others to clear the tables. He dropped the bowls with a clatter as he reached out a tentacle towards the map.

"Err, yes," Comet blustered. "But keep it a secret, there's a good lad, Barney. We don't want every scoundrel aboard knowing about it."

Barney mimed zipping his beak shut. "You can count on me, Captain!" he said proudly.

"Good." Comet popped the map inside an empty bottle of grum for safe-keeping. "By my reckoning, it shouldn't be too long before old Comet here is known as the greatest pirate to have ever sailed the Seven Suns!"

"Where have you been, you hopeless snark? This is no time for moon-watching," shouted Pegg as Sam appeared on deck. "Get over here! And be sharp about it or you'll find out what happened to the last cabin boy!"

Sam found the two-headed first mate really scary – well, half of the first mate, anyway. He hurried over as fast as he could.

"What *did* happen to the last cabin boy?" asked Sam nervously.

"Ah, well, ermm, he's sort of indisposed,"

Legg muttered.

Pegg gave a sinister cackle. "Yeah," he said. "*Permanently* indisposed."

"Anyway," said Legg, cutting in, "cabin boy is a wonderful job full of excitement and possibilities – so make the most of it!"

"Great – so what first?" asked Sam eagerly.

"Well, me hearty, you have the excitement and possibilities of cleaning the ship," sneered Pegg, pushing a mop into Sam's hand. "I want this deck to sparkle. Now, get cracking!"

Sam looked with dismay at the spaceship. If the *Jolly Apollo* had looked dirty from the side of the dock, then up close it was positively filthy. Dirt was ingrained in the deck and the only places where you couldn't see the muck was where food had been spilled. And there were spacegull droppings *everywhere*. It was going to be a long morning.

Three hours later Sam was still cleaning. With a grunt he scraped the last bit of spacegull poo off the top of the crow's nest. It was the worst job

he had ever done in his life and he ached all over – but as he picked up the crow's-nest telescope he couldn't help grinning. A few short hours ago he was listening to Professor Argon droning on and now he was the cabin boy on a real-life pirate ship! Sam could barely believe it.

He had a great view from the crow's nest, too. To his right was the fiery planet of Infernos. To his left the spiral arms of the distant galaxy Busella looked like a boomerang frozen in time, mid-spin. All around were countless other stars, planets and a ship – a spaceship!

"Ship ahoy!" Sam shouted, hoping that was the right thing to say.

"What type is it?" called Captain Comet from the deck.

"It's big," Sam replied, "and coming this way – fast. Hold on a moment..." Sam paused as he fumbled with the telescope, "... it's the *Gravity's Revenge*!"

The news sent the crew down below into a panic. "Hoist the main sails and ready the laser cannons!" shouted Comet. "No – lower the sails and engines full power! Oh my life, it's Black-Hole Beard!"

The crew ran this way and that, bashing into each other and dropping stuff all over the deck – which other people then tripped over. While some of the pirates began hoisting the sails, others were trying to let them down. It was chaos. Sam scurried down from the crow's nest to try and help.

"Don't panic! Don't panic!" cried Comet, clearly panicking himself. "Remember the pirate code! Ready the laser cannon and fire a shot wide of the *Revenge* to welcome a fellow pirate."

BAZOOM!

The *Gravity's Revenge* beat them to it – but their shot went tearing through the *Apollo*'s front mast, toppling half of it on to the deck.

"Well, that was a bit careless!" huffed Comet. "We only just fixed that."

BAZOOM! BAZOOM! BAZOOM!

More shots from *Revenge* went zinging into

the *Jolly Apollo*.

"I don't think that was an accident, Captain!" shouted Sam.

Comet dived behind the main mast, his hat pulled down over his ears.

"Can we fight them off?" shouted Sam.

"Of course we can't!" wailed Comet. "And with our foresail gone there's no way we can outrun them."

With a sickening crunch the *Gravity's Revenge* smashed into the side of the *Jolly Apollo*. Black-Hole Beard's pirates swarmed over the side like angry ants, shouting and cursing, cutlasses waving and space muskets firing. And at the head of them was Black-Hole Beard himself, his sharp laser cutlass glinting cruelly and his foul parrot, Baggot, squawking at his shoulder.

The *Apollo*'s crew tried fighting back, sparks flying as laser cutlass hit laser cutlass, but it was hopeless – the crew of the *Revenge* outnumbered those of the *Jolly Apollo* and they were meaner and keener for the fight. In less than five minutes it was over. Black-Hole Beard had captured the *Jolly Apollo*.

# Chapter Eight

# MAP ATTACK!

Black-Hole Beard glared at the captured crew of the *Jolly Apollo*.

"Now, where's that snivelling whelp you call a captain?" he bellowed.

"I'm here!" said Comet, stepping out from behind the mast and trying to stop his voice from shaking. "How dare you board my ship! It's totally against the pirate code!"

"Squarrr!" screeched Baggot. "What a loser! What a loser!"

"I demand you and your filthy fleabag crew depart – immediately!" continued Comet, giving Baggot a dirty look.

"Now, now, Joseph, there's no need to be like that," said Black-Hole Beard in a wheedling voice. "It's only a social call. It seems we've drunk all our grum, so we've decided to borrow some of yours. Of course, when I say 'borrow' I mean 'take'; and when I say 'some' I mean 'all' – but you get the idea. Right, boys – empty the hold."

"I demand you stop immediately or I'll..."

"Or you'll what?" growled Black-Hole Beard, glaring at Comet.

"Carrr! He's got greasy locks and he wears smelly socks – it's Comet, it's Comet," sang Baggot.

The crew of the *Gravity's Revenge* cackled evilly, slapping each other on the back and shouting unpleasant curses.

Comet's moustache drooped. Barney placed a reassuring tentacle on his shoulder.

"You may mock," he said, "but you'll be laughing on the other side of your faces when we find Planet X!"

The *Revenge*'s crew erupted into gales of laughter. "Oh, not this again," cried Black-Hole Beard.

"As... if... *you*," one pirate gasped, doubled over with laughter, "could find Planet X!"

"We will!" shouted Barney.

"Barney – shush now!" Comet hissed at him.

"Yeah, laugh away," continued Barney.

"Shush!" Comet hissed again.

"But, Captain," said Barney in a loud whisper. "We will! Now you've got that map showing *exactly* where it is."

Suddenly everything was quiet, except for the sound of Comet slapping his hand to his face in despair.

"Uh-oh," said Barney, stuffing a tentacle into

his beak.

"Map, eh?" said Black-Hole Beard. "Why, thank you, Barney." He turned to his grinning crew and waved his hand in the air. "Tear this ship apart, boys, and find that map!"

Sam looked at Captain Comet in despair. *Surely he'd have found a safe hiding place? He must have a safe, or a treasure chest, or a loose floorboard that no one would ever look under...*

"Got it!" one of Black-hold Beard's crew shouted, holding up the grum bottle with the map in it. "It was in his sock drawer."

Black-Hole Beard took it from him and laughed out loud. "A message in a bottle, me hearties," he cried.

Sam stepped towards the front of the crowd. He had to get the map! As the crew of *Gravity's Revenge* cheered, Sam saw his chance and lunged at Black-Hole Beard.

But as he jumped, a heavy hand landed on his shoulder. Then a lobster claw nipped round his waist and pulled him back.

"What are you doing? Let me go!" wailed Sam as Comet's crew surrounded him, standing between him and Black-Hole Beard. Sam struggled desperately, but he was held too tight.

"Shhhhh," whispered Legg as Black-Hole Beard turned in their direction, holding the bottle up high. Sam gulped as the evil pirate's cold eyes stared right through him.

"Control your crew, Comet," he snarled. "Or I'll control them for you. Now, a map like this needs to be with some proper pirates, don't ya think? I don't be supposing you'll do anything as stupid as trying to follow us, but as there's no accounting for just how bone-headed you can be, I'll take a few precautions. Scar! Crank!"

Two hideously ugly pirates leapt to attention.

"Make sure the *Apollo*'s engines are missing some vital parts," instructed Black-Hole Beard.

"Aye aye, Cap'n!" they sneered. A couple of moments later they returned with some greasy bits of metal.

"Well done, lads – now chuck 'em overboard," yelled Black-Hole Beard. "C'mon me hearties – we've treasure to find!"

Black-Hole Beard and his crew swept back to their ship, Baggot squawking a rude song about

the *Jolly Apollo* and toilets. *Gravity's Revenge* blasted off with a deafening roar and was gone.

The crew of the *Jolly Apollo* watched in silence as their enemies disappeared into the vastness of space.

"That's that, then," said Comet. Then, turning on his heel, he marched back to his cabin and slammed the door.

Sam turned to the pirates angrily. "My parents are stranded on Planet X," he yelled. "*That's* how I got the map. And now it's gone and there's no way I'll ever be able to rescue them. Why did you stop me?"

"Because we prefer you alive," replied Legg.

"Yeah, if anyone's going to kill our cabin boy, it's going to be us," said Pegg grumpily, before joining the rest of their crewmates as they began to drift slowly and silently downstairs.

"The ghost of Long John Starseeker," one muttered as he went below deck. "Yeah, right." An air of deep gloom descended over the ship.

Sam wandered to the side of the ship and

stared into the black emptiness of space. All was quiet apart from the creaking of the rigging as the *Apollo*'s remaining sails caught the solar winds that carried the ship along. He felt tears burning his eyes and blinked them away. There was a tap on his shoulder. Sam turned round to find Barney standing there. Sam had found him terrifying before, but now the Kraken just looked sheepish, twisting his tentacles awkwardly as he looked at Sam.

"I'm really sorry," Barney mumbled. "Sometimes my beak moves quicker than my brain."

Barney looked so miserable that Sam didn't want to make him feel worse. "It's all right," he mumbled. "I know you didn't mean to."

There was an awkward silence as they both looked out into space. Sam watched a crumpled silver bag float past.

"What's that?" he asked.

"Oh, that'll be Black-Hole Beard chucking his rubbish overboard again," said Barney. "It's

disgusting! I mean, look at all that!" Barney pointed a tentacle at more floating rubbish.

Sam stared at the litter, then leaned over the side to get a better look. There was one bit after another, all bobbing gently in space in a long line. A long line leading straight to *Gravity's Revenge*!

"Barney, you're a genius!" shouted Sam.

"I am?" said Barney.

"Yes – don't you see? Black-Hole Beard has left a trail that will lead us right to him!"

Barney smiled slowly as Sam's words sank in.

"I *am* a genius," he said quietly, looking very proud.

"Barney, go and tell the captain that we need to get those boosters fixed!" said Sam. "The race to Planet X isn't over yet!"

# Chapter Nine
# JUNGRUM

"**S**trike!" yelled Barney, as Sam's ball zoomed down the lane and smashed over all of the hovering pins. Sam grinned as the other pirates on his team clustered around him and cheered. Almost a whole deck in the belly of the ship was filled with a giant bowling alley, and there were always some pirates there having a game. Sam had never bowled much before, but the pirates' enthusiasm was infectious. Better still, it turned out that he was quite good, and after a couple of lucky shots everyone wanted him to be on their team.

Over the last few days the *Jolly Apollo* had raced ahead, following the rubbish trail through asteroid storms, past flaming comets and by planets of all shapes and sizes. But they hadn't seen *Gravity's Revenge*. Sam had quickly got used to life as cabin boy on board a space-pirate ship. Already he could scrub the decks clean of spacegull poo and still have time for a game of bowling before lunch.

Sam glanced round at the rest of his team. He'd

got to know the crew over the last few days as well. The jelly-bodied pirate, Slurp, was always grumpy, the hairy creature, Piole, actually had twelve mouths, and the fearsome-looking Snippernaut, Romero, turned out to be a bit of a comedian.

As Sam watched, Romero grabbed a bowling ball in his claws and pretended that it was too heavy to lift. Sam was just about to take his next shot when there was a cry from the deck above.

"Ship ahoy! It's the *Revenge*!"

Sam and the others stampeded up to the deck. "It looks deserted, Cap'n," said Legg as he peered through the telescope.

"Hoist the sails!" shouted Comet. "Boosters to dock speed. Easy to starboard, we'll moor up behind that asteroid."

"Aye aye, sir!" came the replies.

The *Jolly Apollo* eased into the cover of a large asteroid that was orbiting a small planet.

"*Gravity's Revenge* will never spot us here!" said Comet happily.

Sam peered curiously over the side at the planet below. *Maybe that was where Black-Hole Beard and his crew were?*

"Right, me lads, the plan is to sneak aboard and look for that map while the *Revenge* is deserted," said Comet.

"What if Black-Hole Beard has the map with him? Surely he'd never leave something so important behind?" asked Sam.

"Ah, yes," said Comet. "Ahem. As I was about to say before I was so rudely interrupted, the plan is to sneak on board the *Revenge* once we've already confirmed that Black-Hole Beard hasn't got the map on him. So *first*, we should go down to that planet. Pegg, Legg, what can you see?"

The two-headed first mate was fighting over the ship telescope.

"It's my turn!" snapped Pegg.

"I think you'll find it's mine," said Legg.

"Mine!" snapped Pegg.

"Mine!" squealed Legg.

"*Mine!*" sighed Comet, pushing his first mate

out of the way.

Comet placed his eye to the telescope. "Oh I say! Would you look at that!" he said, dancing around with his eye still pressed to the lens.

"What can you see, Captain?" asked Sam as Comet giggled to himself.

"Well, the surface is covered in jungle and large, yellow lakes. Which means I know exactly where we are," Comet replied excitedly.

"It's not—" gasped Slurp.

"It *is*, my fine, furry friend! That's the planet Jungrum – and those are the galaxy-famous grum lakes! Fetch any empty containers you can lay your hands on; we're going down for supplies!"

There was a huge cheer.

"Load the empty bottles and barrels into the shuttle," ordered Comet. "I'll take Barney, and Pegg and Legg with me."

"Great!" said Barney. "I'll bring a picnic!"

"Hey, what about me?" shouted Sam above the din. "It was my map in the first place!"

"Oh, all right," said Comet. "You're only small

– but if you take up valuable grum space I'm leaving you there."

When Sam clambered aboard the shuttle he was disappointed to see that it was basically just a rowing boat with rocket boosters on the oars. The shuttle was so crammed with empty bottles, bowls and buckets – and anything else that would hold grum – that Sam had to sit inside a barrel.

"Hold tight," yelled Barney, grabbing all four of the shuttle's oars. "Yum, grum, here we come!"

The Kraken gave the oars a heave, the boosters burst into life and they set off at blistering speed, trailing sparks like a firework through the sky.

"Phew! That's some rowing boat!" gasped Sam, struggling to his feet.

"Fastest one this side of Spabula galaxy!" said Barney. "There are buttons on the handles to control the speed and you move the oars to change direction."

The boat was so quick that by the time Barney had

finished explaining how the shuttle worked they
had landed.

Captain Comet climbed out of the boat and had
a quick look at the dense vegetation all around
them. "This way!" he said, stalking off through
the undergrowth, his coat flapping.

"How does he know where Black-Hole Beard
will be?" Sam asked as he struggled out
of his barrel.

"If there's one thing
the captain's good at, it's
pretending he knows what he's doing,"
replied Legg.

"And that's the *only* thing he's good at,"
added Pegg.

The jungle was hot and steamy and the plants
were difficult to fight through, even with Barney
at the front. He was doing a great job of making
a path through the vegetation by chomping on
the thick blue leaves and slimy jungle vines.
Sam stared in disbelief as yet another tentacleful
of leaves went into his beak. But although
Barney's belly was big, the jungle was
much, much bigger.

"Stop!" cried Comet suddenly,
standing dead still.

Sam watched as the captain
went cross-eyed. He seemed
to be staring down
at his own nose.

"What's wrong?" asked Sam.

"His moustache is twitching," whispered Legg.

"Is that a bad thing?" asked Sam.

"That's always a bad thing," warned Pegg.

"HHHEEEELLLLLPPPPPPP!"

The shout shattered the silence. For a moment the pirates stood staring at each other.

"Let's go!" said Sam.

"Yes," agreed Comet. "Back to the shuttle, men!"

"No, I mean let's go and *help*!" said Sam.

"Oh, of course," said Comet. "Barney, chomp in that direction! Pirates to the rescue!"

Chapter Ten

# RESCUE MISSION

The pirates went crashing through the jungle as fast as Barney could eat a pathway. Branches grabbed at their clothes and spiky leaves tore at their faces. Then they were through, tumbling out of the dense wall of plants and on to the wide shore of a lake with fizzy, lemon-yellow waters that stretched out into the distance.

With a whoop and cheer the pirates ran headlong into the foamy waters. All except Sam, who stood in amazement as the pirates splashed around filling up bottles, barrels and even their hats with grum, laughing like lunatics.

"Come on!" shouted Sam. "That can wait! What about the person who was shouting for help?"

Captain Comet spat a mouthful of grum from his mouth in a long arc like a fountain.

"What *are* you talking about?" he said.

"HHHHEEEEEELLLLLLLLLPPPPPPP!"

"*That!*" said Sam.

Moaning and looking longingly at the grum, the pirates squelched out of the lake and followed

Sam along the shore.

"Look," he said.

In the middle of the next grum lake there was a small island with a group of people huddled on it – and not just any people, but Black-Hole Beard and his crew! Sam tried not to laugh when he saw them. They must have been swimming in the grum, because they were all wearing bathing costumes. Black-Hole Beard had a full-body red and white stripy one and swimming hat with a skull and cross-rockets on the sides. His Minocerous first mate, Yarr, was wearing armbands, and at least three other pirates had rubber rings and inflatables. And they were all doing their best to be as far away as possible from the grum lake. As they were on a tiny island this involved lots of pushing and shoving.

"I wonder what they're so worried about?" said Comet, going right up to the shoreline to get a good look.

"Look out!" cried Barney, wrapping the captain in a tentacle and jerking him away from the lake.

Just in time – a bright-blue creature with five eyes and a long snout like a crocodile burst from the surface, its snapping jaws just missing the curly end of Comet's moustache. It disappeared back beneath the yellow waves with a huge splash. The captain turned deathly pale and clutched at his moustache.

"This lake's infested with grumigators!" said Legg. "No wonder that motley lot on the island are so scared."

The splash had caught the attention of the *Revenge*'s crew, who started waving and calling them.

"Captain Comet – thank the stars you've come!" cried Black-Hole Beard. "I always knew you'd track us down sooner or later!"

"Liar!" Comet replied. "You pinched our map and grum and left us adrift!"

"Ah, that was just my little joke, Joseph. No hard feelings," continued Black-Hole Beard, attempting a friendly smile and failing.

A grumigator fin broke the surface and swam

94

past the island, causing one of the *Revenge*'s biggest, hairiest pirates to scream like a little girl.

"Well, this is *my* little joke," said Comet. "We're off! Come on, me hearties, let's fill our bottles and go."

"Arrr, Comet, matey! You can't leave us here like this – it's against the pirate code!" cried Black-Hole Beard.

Comet stopped in his tracks.

"Don't fall for that, Captain; you know what he thinks of the code," snapped Pegg.

"But the code's the code!" whispered Comet.

"Enough about the code!" cried Sam. "Look, he's got the map in a grum bottle around his neck! We've *got* to help him."

Even Pegg couldn't grumble with that.

"OK, Black-Hole Beard, we'll help you, but we want our map back!" called Comet.

"Deal!" replied Black-Hole Beard as another grumigator glided past.

"Right, where's your shuttle?" asked Comet.

"It sank." Black-Hole Beard pointed at the

remains of a boat poking out of the grum. The rest of his pirates started shuffling their feet and looking shamefaced. "There was a bit of a scuffle when we saw the grumigators, see, and..."

Sam grinned. "You all panicked so much you capsized?"

"Aye," admitted Black-Hole Beard.

When the crew of the *Jolly Apollo* had stopped laughing, which took a long time, Comet agreed to go and fetch their shuttle. "Wait there," he told Black-Hole Beard, sniggering.

A grumigator swam lazily past the stricken pirates.

"Believe me," Black-Hole Beard said with a sigh. "We're not going anywhere."

***

It took a while to struggle back through the jungle with the shuttle.

"Why couldn't we have flown it back here?" asked Sam.

"Because we've only got enough fuel for the

journey back to the *Apollo*," explained Legg.

"What kept you?" barked Black-Hole Beard.

"Don't push your luck," Comet replied, mopping his brow. "Now, who's rowing across? I can't go obviously; I'm too important. And Barney can't go as he's the cook..."

"Like we'd miss his cooking," said Pegg under his breath.

"....and Pegg and Legg would only argue," continued Comet. "Which leaves you, Sam. Good luck!"

"What?" exclaimed Sam. "You lot are unbelievable!"

The pirates pushed the shuttle into the water and Pegg chucked Sam on board.

Sam slowly sculled across the lake. Every so often a grumigator would appear, watching the shuttle hungrily.

"C'mon, c'mon," said Black-Hole Beard impatiently as the boat edged closer.

"Map first," Sam demanded, holding out his hand.

Black-Hole Beard scowled as he handed over the grum bottle. Sam loosened the cork and peered inside. He could see the familiar scrap of silver spacesuit and felt a warm wave of relief. He stoppered the bottle and shoved it inside his top.

"OK, welcome aboard," said Sam.

The *Revenge*'s crew piled into the boat. Sam got bashed and pushed as the pirates squeezed on and forced him further and further up the shuttle. Eventually he found himself jammed in Yarr's armpit at the very head of the boat. Black-Hole Beard surveyed the scene from the middle of the shuttle as the last pirate struggled to get on.

# Stowaway!

"It's a bit cramped in here, Mr Yarr," said Black-Hole Beard with a knowing nod at Sam.

"Arr!" replied Yarr. Before Sam had time to react, the Minocerous pushed him out of the boat and into the lake.

"Man overboard!" cackled Black-Hole Beard. "Here, give me ye hand and I'll help you in."

Coughing and spluttering, Sam reached up.

"But I'll have ye map first," said Black-Hole Beard with an evil grin.

"No way!" shouted Sam.

"Well, then you can take your chances with the grumigators," laughed Black-Hole Beard.

Slowly, Sam rummaged in his pockets and held up the grum bottle. Black-Hole Beard snatched it. Sam put up his hand for Black-Hole Beard to pull him in, but the pirate captain turned his back on him.

"Right, me hearties, let's get back to the *Revenge*," commanded Black-Hole Beard.

"You dirty, double-crossing, no-good lowlife!" shouted Sam.

"Save your energy for swimming," sneered Black-Hole Beard. "Thanks for the shuttle, Comet!"

"Carrr," squawked Baggot. "Sucker! Sucker!"

The shuttle spun round in the water. In a shower of grum it blasted up into the air, leaving Sam in the lake.

Sam looked towards the shore – and a set of five grumigator eyes stared straight back at him.

# Chapter Eleven
# STRANDED!

SPACE PIRATES

"That's not in the pirate code!" shrieked Comet indignantly.

"Erm, a little help here, please," Sam called nervously, keeping his eyes on the grumigator ahead of him. The grum trickled down his face and into his mouth. Even in his dangerous situation Sam couldn't help but think how delicious it was.

"Sam!" shouted Barney. "Use your tentacles and swim for it!"

"I haven't got tentacles!" replied Sam, panicking. He started to swim as fast as he could, sure that the deadly jaws of a grumigator would close round him at any moment.

Then a shadow moved through the water in front of him, and a spiky fin surfaced. "HELP!" Sam yelled, as the open mouth of the grumigator appeared before him. Suddenly a sandwich splashed into the water next to the grumigator, and it lunged for that instead of Sam.

"Oh, good shot, Barney!" yelled Comet.

On the far shore, Barney was throwing his picnic sandwiches from every tentacle. The grumigators snapped them up as soon as they hit the water. "At least someone appreciates my cooking!" the Kraken yelled.

"Sam, quick!" shouted Comet.

"I haven't got many sandwiches left!" added Barney.

Sam swam faster than he knew he could. He was still a good way from the shore when Barney yelled, "That's the last one!" and launched a sandwich into the grum.

Sam risked a look over his shoulder. Behind him, the lake boiled as the grumigators finished off the sandwiches and looked around for their next snack. Sam gulped, then he kicked his legs as if his life depended on it – because it did. Suddenly he felt himself hauled the last couple of metres on to the shore, wrapped in Barney's tentacles. The angry snapping of jaws from the lake told Sam just how close he had come to being the latest ex-cabin boy of the *Jolly Apollo*.

Sam wobbled unsteadily to his feet. He was drenched to his skin and the fizzy grum had given him terrible hiccups and a sudden desire to go bowling. "Thank you, Barney," said Sam, alarmed to find himself close to tears now the danger had passed.

"If you start blubbing," threatened Pegg, "I'm throwing you back in the lake."

"Captain, how are we going to get back now Black-Hole Beard has pinched our shuttle?" said Legg.

"Don't worry, your trusty captain will come up

with an answer," replied Comet.

There was a long silence in which Comet stroked his moustache and hummed and hawed a lot.

"We need to alert the *Jolly Apollo*," said Sam weakly.

"Exactly! I was just about to say that," said Comet.

"And how do we do that, Captain?" asked Barney. "The communicators won't work down here."

"Erm... we... err... well... you tell 'em, Sam," said Comet.

Sam looked around and grabbed a long blue sticky vine. "Maybe we could make a message big enough for them to see from space." He laid out the vine on the dusty floor. "Use anything we

can to spell the word 'HELP' – the bigger the better."

"Precisely!" said Comet. "Really, Barney, a fool could have worked that out. Right, me hearties, let's get to work. Everyone grab some vines."

Spelling out a simple message took a lot longer than Sam thought it would. The vines were tricky to chop and withered in the heat of the sun. It was hot and frustrating work and after half an hour they still didn't have enough to make the letter "H".

"This is a stupid idea!" complained Pegg.

"And I suppose you've got a better one?" replied Legg.

Sam slumped to the floor for a rest and watched them argue. They were still at it when Barney turned up carrying three unconscious grumigators.

"Wow, Barney – how did you knock them out?" asked Sam.

"I think it might have been the sandwiches,"

Barney said sadly. "They've gone all floppy."

"Hey, we could use them to spell out our message!" said Sam. "Are there any more?"

"There's plenty of them floating in the lake," smiled Barney.

Within five minutes Barney was back and had spelled out "HELP" in large grumigator letters. Pegg and Legg were still too busy arguing to notice, but Comet looked up from where he'd been taking a sneaky snooze.

"Arr, good work, me hearties!" he said. "An extra ration of grum for you when we get back on board! Now then, let's hope there's someone on the *Apollo* using the telescope."

"And let's hope they get here before these grumigators wake up," added Sam.

# Chapter Twelve

# TO PLANET X!

Sam stared into the sky, waiting for some kind of sign that the *Jolly Apollo* had seen the message.

"Perhaps it's too small," he wondered aloud.

"Maybe it's not spelled right," said Pegg.

"Of course it's spelled right," snapped Legg, and immediately they started arguing again.

"Oh, give me strength," sighed Comet.

"Shhhhhh!" Sam hissed, looking down at the grumigators. One of them was moving. Everyone went very quiet as the grumigator's tail twitched. Then its mouth opened and it gave a huge, echoing burp.

"Shiver me laser beams, the beast's awake!" whispered Comet, staring at the grumigator's sharp purple teeth. "What *is* that cursed crew doing? Where is the *Apollo*?"

One by one the grumigators began to shuffle about, burping noisily.

"I don't think they liked the sandwiches," said Barney as one rolled around, groaning.

"No kidding, Beaky!" hissed Pegg.

"Who are you calling Beaky, Two Heads?"

snapped Barney.

"Hey, leave me out of this!" shouted Legg.

"Someone *do* something," Comet said in a panic. "Cabin Boy, any bright ideas?"

"Look!" said Sam.

"I *am* looking! That's how I know they're waking up! Can't you do better than that?" snapped Comet.

"No, *look*," said Sam, pointing upwards.

A streak of light was heading straight for them.

"It's the *Apollo*!" cried Legg.

"About time too," said Comet.

Suddenly a large basket hanging from a rope dropped down in front of them.

"We won't all fit in that," said Sam.

"It's for the grum," explained Barney.

"Typical!" sniffed Comet. "Their captain is in mortal danger and all they're worried about is the grum!"

Just then a rope ladder unfurled in front of them.

"Good, good! Women and captains first," said

Comet, grabbing a bottle of grum and jumping on to the ladder. "Make sure all that grum gets loaded while you're at it."

The remaining pirates quickly chucked the grum into the basket and headed up the ladder as fast as their legs and tentacles could carry them.

Although the crew was glad everyone, and the grum, was back on board, the mood went flat when they heard that Black-Hole Beard had double-crossed them.

"So, me hearties, it looks like Black-Hole Beard will find Planet X after all. He'll be even more famous and we'll still be nothing," Comet sighed.

The crew let the news sink in.

"Sorry about your mum and dad," said Barney, laying a rubbery tentacle softly on Sam's shoulder. "Perhaps Black-Hole Beard will rescue them – he might release them for a ransom."

"You don't look too upset about it, lad," said Comet.

"Why should I," said Sam gleefully, "when I've got this!" He reached inside his shirt and pulled out the grum bottle containing the map. "I gave Black-Hole Beard an empty bottle from the shuttle," he explained.

"The old grum-bottle switcheroo!" cried Comet proudly. "Arrr, I'll make a pirate of you yet! I think that deserves a game and a grum! Last one to the bowling alley's a glugspawn egg!"

The crew of the *Apollo* cheered. But just then the large telescreen at the front of the ship crackled into life and Black-Hole Beard's angry face filled the screen.

"Curse you, Comet! I don't know how you did it, you snivelling planet-lubber, but no one gets away with double-crossing me! I'm coming for that map, and when I catch you I'm going to feed your guts to the space gulls; I'm going to—"

Comet switched off the telescreen.

"Oh, has he gone? We must be getting terrible reception behind this asteroid," said Comet. "I really should get a new antenna."

The crew laughed and cheered.

"Now, where was I?" mused Comet. "Ah yes! Thanks to our new cabin boy, we have the map that tells us how to find Planet X. Tomorrow we shall set off to rescue Sam's parents and earn our fame and fortune! But tonight... we bowl!" Comet held up his hand until the cheers died down. "A toast. To Sam – the hero of the day!"

"To Sam," responded the crew. "The hero of the day!"

Sam looked at his fellow crew members as they put on their bowling shoes and smiled. *They might be a bit useless*, he thought, *but their hearts are in the right place*. It hardly seemed possible that only a few days ago he was at home, waiting for his parents. When he had looked at all those different pirate ships moored up at the port, he never would have thought that he'd end up on the *Jolly Apollo*. But now he was on a pirate spaceship sailing through unknown galaxies full of exciting planets – and right there, right then it felt like the best place to be in the entire universe.

Tomorrow he would set off to find his parents – and who knew what else!

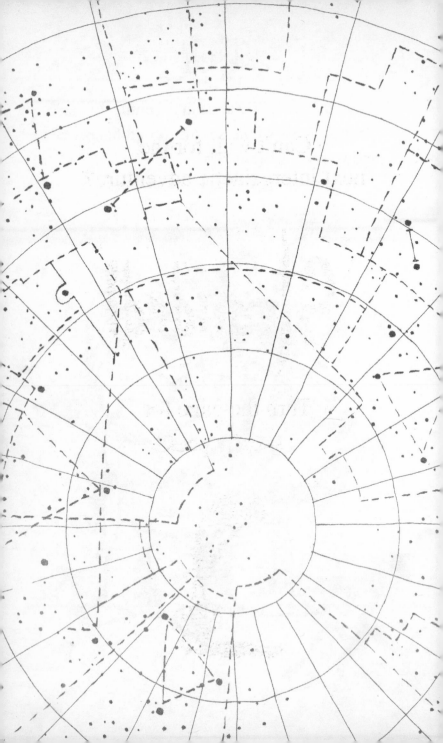

Can't wait for the
next intergalactic adventure?

# Stranded!

Turn the page for
a sneaky peek!

# Chapter One
## SHADOWED!

# Stranded!

"Full speed ahead!" Sam yelled.

The large sails of the spaceship *Jolly Apollo* filled with the solar winds gusting from the bright-orange sun ahead of it and tacked gracefully across the empty space of the Auroran solar system. The *Jolly Apollo* was no ordinary spaceship – it was a pirate ship! It was also a patched-up wreck crewed by an assorted bunch of aliens who were quite possibly the most useless space pirates the galaxy had ever seen. All apart from one: the new cabin boy, Samson Starbuck.

"That's it! That's Lumiere Max!" said Sam, pointing at a nearby sun.

"Batten your hatch there, shipmate. Some of us are trying to get a well-earned rest," replied Captain Comet.

Comet was the captain of the *Apollo*. He was tall, thin and three-eyed (though eye patches covered two of his eyes), with a magnificent waxed moustache. Dressed in a long frock coat and tricorn hat, he looked every inch the perfect pirate. Unfortunately, Comet's dress sense was

the most pirate-like thing about him. At that precise moment he was lounging in a chair with a pair of three-lensed sunglasses perched on his nose and a foaming glass of grum in his hand.

Grum was the drink of choice for pirates – a kind of foamy lemonade that encouraged bowling and kept space scurvy away.

"But, Captain," Sam insisted, "Lumiere Max is on my parent's map!"

Sam's parents had been spaceship-wrecked on the legendary Planet X, but had managed to use their ship's homing beacon to send Sam a map, scribbled on a piece of spacesuit material.

The little planet where Sam and his parents lived was a barren rock in the middle of nowhere, with nothing on it apart from his parent's lab and a port full of vicious space pirates. Luckily, the only thing space pirates love more than bowling is treasure, and every pirate had heard the rumours of Planet X – a lost planet made of solid gold. When Sam had shown Captain Comet the map, he'd been welcomed aboard as the newest member of the *Jolly Apollo*'s crew.

"Lumiere Max? Are you sure?" asked Comet, suddenly interested.

He fished around inside his coat and pulled out the scrap of silvery spacesuit material the map was drawn on. Pushing his sunglasses up on to his head he peered at it intently. He blinked, and then – making sure no one was looking – flicked up his eye patches to reveal two perfectly good eyes. He stared again at the map.

"Well, blow down me main braces, that's right!" Comet muttered to himself. He flipped his patches back down and cleared his throat. "Well done, Sam. I wondered when you'd spot it. I'd noticed it myself ages ago, of course."

Across the deck, Barney the ship's cook – a huge, multi-tentacled squid-like alien – grinned and rolled his eyes at Comet's boastful ways...